Pirate's Peril

Compatible with

The 9th Age™

Impressum:

Written by the T9A Team

Published by FlorianGressConsulting, Rosenweg 24, 93053 Regensburg, Germany

Printed by Amazon Media EU S.à r.l., 5 Rue Plaetis, L-2338, Luxembourg

ISBN: 978-3-98807-003-6

THE IX AGE
FANTASY BATTLES

Pirate's Peril

A T9A SKIRMISH GAME

Designed by Jan Willem "Blonde Beer" Veenhof

The Archipelago of Tartaga	*Page 3*
Pirates Peril Introduction	*Page 4*
Basic Setup of the Game	*Page 4*
Building your Pirate Band	*Page 5*
Pregame Actions	*Page 6*
Playing the Game	*Page 8*
Movement Phase	*Page 8*
Shooting Phase	*Page 9*
Close Combat Phase	*Page 10*
Playing a Campaign	*Page 13*
Greenhide Pirate Band	*Page 16*
Vampire Pirate Band	*Page 19*
Dwarf Pirate Band	*Page 21*
Human Pirate Band	*Page 23*
Elven Pirate Band	*Page 25*
Ogre Pirate Band	*Page 27*
Character sheets	*Page 29*
Building your Pirate Table	*Page 31*

The Story of Pirate's Peril:

The Dreaded Pirate Lord

The story of Pirate's Peril is all about your own band of pirates facing other groups of pirates for a chance to find treasure. But before we get to the fun we have to start at the beginning, and the story of Pirates Peril begins with the Dreaded Pirate Lord Putnam Darkwalker. Putnam started his career as a regular Arcalean Merchant Captain, until one day he took on board a strange passenger on one of his voyages. Details are sparse and the subject of many tavern tales, but after this voyage he abandoned his duty and became known as the Pirate Putnam Darkwalker.

Few pirates set sail after dusk, let alone strike at heavy vessels, but Darkwalker made his name striking in deepest night and escaping by dawn with spoils enough to buy a kingdom. In the years that followed his reputation grew along with his fleet, and many dark stories followed his attacks. After a while he was no longer just a Pirate Captain, but a King among Pirates, or, as he became known, the Dreaded Pirate Lord.

Indeed, so many other pirate captains were drawn by his success that towns and harbours sprang up all across the Archipelago, striking from there at shipping routes between Vetia, Taphria and Silexia. In those times, all feared for Tartaga's growing strength, for even it was on the verge of becoming its own nation with Putnam as Pirate King.

The Feast of Blood and Pillage and the Great Wave

Yet all that is won is not always golden, for at the peak of their might on the eve of their annual revel, a disaster struck. From the depths of the Shattered Sea came a storm unlike any seen for over a century. Some say the magic that birthed it made it impossible for weather readers and mystics to predict. Others claim the jealous Dark Gods themselves sent it as punishment for the collective sins of Tartaga. Whatever the reason, with the storm came the Great Wave, a tsunami that crashed down upon the Archipelago like a new Skyhammer.

When the waters ebbed away and light returned, everything had changed. Tartaga had become a cemetery for pirates and ships alike. Throughout the islands and islets, wrecks litter beaches and coves, with some half buried in the sands along with their amassed hordes. Now, a handful of years later, rumours of treasures, and the chance to claim some of the splendor of Darkwalker's empire, are drawing new pirates and rogues to Tartaga.

Among these devastated towns, beaches, harbors and shipwrecks can be found the new wave of brave pirates, sneaking buccaneers and vicious marauders; Clashing and fighting as each seeks their share of the gold and glory, and to survive the Pirate's Peril.

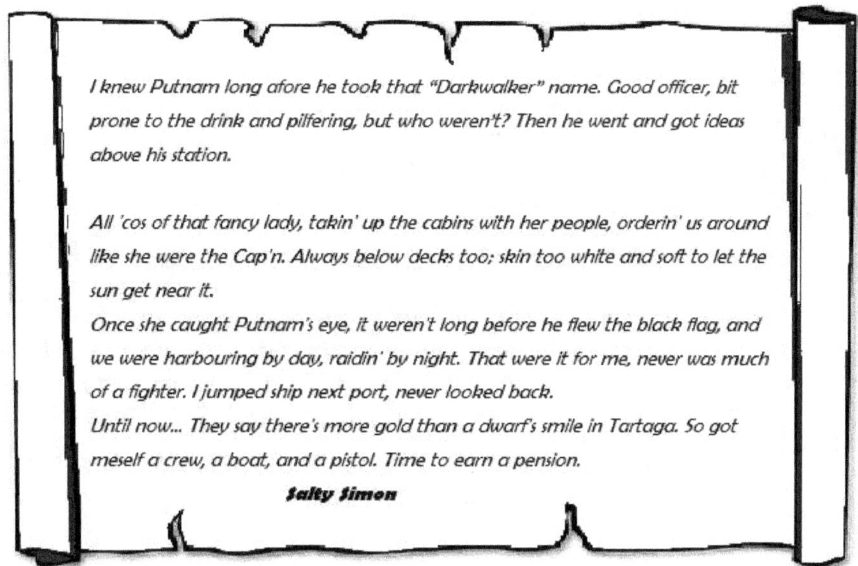

Pirate's Peril

Introduction:

Pirate's Peril is at its core is a simplified version of the basic The 9th Age: Fantasy Battles ruleset, but with 2 major changes.

First, the focus has been moved from fighting massive battles between armies, into a small skirmish game, where bands of different kinds of pirates and buccaneers fight in the streets of the deserted archipelago of Tartaga, looking to claim treasure left there.

The second big change is that the main rules have been simplified to create a game that is easy to pick up for younger or new players, and is there for a great introduction game for them. The focus is on fast, fun, and furious gameplay that we hope you and your opponent will enjoy!

Basic Setup of the Game:

A game of Pirate's Peril consists of the following parts:
1. Building a Pirate Band   (See page 5)
2. Playing the game, and fighting with your Pirates   (See page 8)
3. Post battle Calculations (and if using a campaign, rolling for results). (See Page 13)

Rolling Dice
Certain actions in the game need to be resolved with dice. This game uses the common six-sided die, commonly called a D6, to determine results.

Measuring and Distances
The unit of measurement in Pirate's Peril is the Inch. All distances are measured from the closest parts of any model's base or interacting terrain. You can measure any distance in the game at any moment during the game.

Building your Pirate Band:

Each player must create his or her Pirate Band before playing Pirate's Peril.

Each Pirate Band is created by using golden doubloons as the currency, where each model and each upgrade costs X amount of doubloons. Each Pirate Band must have at least 3 models to start with, and a maximum of 12 models (ogre bands have a maximum of 9 models).

The basic setup for any Pirate Band as a one off game, or as the start for a campaign is as follows:

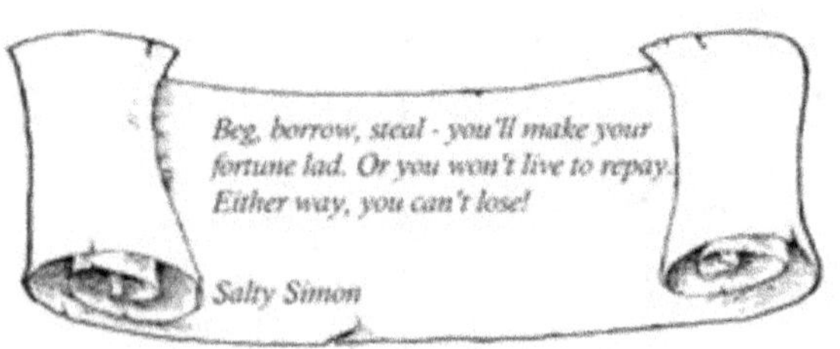

Starting Gold:

Each player can use 200 doubloons in total for creating his Pirate Band. You can use less if you want, and in case of a campaign, the remaining doubloons go your treasure chest. Choose one of the Pirate Band Lists (see page XX). You can only choose models from that Pirate Band List to create your Pirate Band.

Hiring Pirates:

The Captain:

Each Pirate Band must be led by a single Captain (and you can only have 1 single Captain).

Besides that can you spend your doubloons in any way you want.

The rest of the Pirate Band:

Pirates are divided in 2 different categories: Officers and Crew Members.

Officers usually have better stats, and gain experience after each game when playing a campaign, but cost more than regular Crew Members. Each Pirate Band may only have 5 officers in total (including the Captain) and a maximum of 10 Pirates in total for most Pirate Bands (unless noted in their Pirate Band List.. A healthy mix of both is the best way to gain success as a pirate!

Equipment:

You must use your doubloons to buy to give your pirates weapons . Any Pirate can only have a maximum of 2 weapons though (any Pair of Weapons counts as 2 weapons).

Special Rules:

Certain models have unique special rules. You can find those in your Pirate Band list and they come standard with your pirate models. Officers can gain experience and either increase their statistics, or they can buy additional Special Rules (see page XX).

Pre-Game Actions

Pregame Setup:

1. Share your Pirate Band Roster with the other player(s)
2. Build the Battlefield and roll for Scenario
3. Determine the Deployment Zones
4. Deployment of models
5. Roll for first turn

Step 1: Share your Pirate Band Roster with the other player(s)
Show your band to the opponent, and answer any questions about equipment, statistics or special rules of the models.

Step 2: Build the Battlefield and roll for Scenario
Have a designated area on the table to play on and both players add terrain to it to simulate a battlefield. Tables can be as big as both players want, but at least 30 by 30 inches is suggested as the minimum size.
After this you can roll for scenario. Have one player roll a D6 and check the table beneath for the scenario:

Dice Roll	Result	Dice Roll	Result
1	Bloodbath	4	Sink the Enemy Ship
3	Treasure A-plenty!	5	Treasure A-plenty!
3	A New Storm	6	Bloodbath

Bloodbath:
While looking for treasure, it becomes clear that there is none to be found, except those on the bodies of the other Pirate Band that appeared. For each enemy model that is mortally wounded you gain a Treasure Token at the end of the Game up to a maximum of 6.

Treasure A-plenty:
Both players roll a D6. The highest roll is the amount of Treasure Tokens that are placed on the board. The player with the highest roll (in case of tie, keep rolling off to see who starts) places the first treasure token on the board, at least 8 inches away from any board edge. The next player places the next token, at least 8 inches away from the board edge, and 8 inches away from any other treasure token. Keep rotating the placing of the tokens between the players until all the tokens are placed. A treasure can be claimed by any model that is in base to base contact with a treasure token at the end of his movement phase. Each model can only carry one treasure token, and if the model is mortally wounded, he drops his token on the board again on the spot he was.
At the end of the game you gain a Treasure Token for each Treasure Token carried by your models.

A New Storm:
The wind is starting to blow harder and harder, bringing fear to even the blackest of pirate heart. It's time to get away as fast as possible, and find shelter, but it's also a good chance to get rid of some of the competition. Both players have to move their models from the start of their deployment zone, and touch the end of the other side of the board. As soon as they touch the board they are removed from the game (safely). Check at the end of the game how many models each player successfully moved of the board. For each model you got to safety more than your opponent you receive a Treasure Token up to a maximum of 6.

Sink the Enemy Ship:
Whenever a pirate ship is docked, it becomes an easy target for attack. Both Players place a Ship Token (see appendix for a paper cut out) on the board touching their deployment zone but at least 2 inches away from any blocking terrain.
You can destroy the enemy's ship by placing one of your models on the Ship Token in your turn. If the model is still alive at the end of the opponent's turn and not in base to base contact with an enemy model, it can light the gunpowder reserves on board, and destroy the ship.
Destroying the opponents ship gives you D3+1 Treasure Tokens at the end of the game.

Monster Hunt:
After the Great Wave not only were there lives and treasures lost, the sea also brought its own gifts to the Archipelago. Place a Monster Model (or use the Token in the Appendix) in the exact middle of the board. If that's not possible try to place it as close as possible. The Monster is hurt though, and can't really move around anymore, but it is sitting next to a big pile of Treasure.
The Monster:

Movement	Strength	Resilience	Attack	Agility	Hitpoints	Aim	Weapon skill
0	5	5	5	1	5	0	3

Whenever the Monster is in base to base contact with any model it will attack in every combat phase (the other player will roll its attack to attack you, and you for him). When the monster dies roll D6 for the amount of Treasure Tokens. Each model within 4 inches of the centre of the location when the monster died can pick up a single treasure token from the body of the Monster. Each model can only carry one treasure token, and if the model is mortally wounded, he drops his token on the board again on the spot he was.

Used to have 2 eyes, 2 legs and a lot more luck with the ladies before I tangled with a Kraken. Still, now I have a crew to do the dirty work."

Salty Simon

At the end of the game you gain a Treasure token for each Treasure Token carried by your models.

When playing a one off game, the one with the most Treasure Tokens wins the game. In case of a draw.. it's a draw!

Step 3 and 4: Determine the Deployment Zones
Both players roll a D6. The one with the highest result may pick an edge of the table (in case of a tie, reroll), and place his models within 4 inches from this edge. The opposing player chooses another table edge to place his models, but they must be at least half the width of the table in inches away from the other players models.

Step 5: Roll for first turn:
Both players roll a D6. The one with the highest result may decide who starts the game (in case of a tie, reroll). If there are more players than 2, the second highest goes second, the third highest goes third etc etc.

Playing the Game

6 Turns of Infamy and Booty!
Pirate's Peril is a turn based game, consisting of 6 Game Turns in total, or when one of the players has no models left on the table that aren't mortally wounded.

In each turn, each player has their own player turn, in the order as decided by the roll for first turn.

When each player has finished their turn, the Game Turn is over, and the next Game Turn starts.

Each player's turn is divided in the following phases:

1. Movement phase
2. Shooting phase
3. Close Combat phase

The Movement Phase

During the movement phase a player can move his or her models around the table. Each model can only take a single movement action, and each model is moved one after another. As soon as a model is moved, it can't be moved again during the movement phase.

Each model has an individual movement value (M). The movement value is the maximum amount in inches that a model can move, and still take other actions, like shooting, or special abilities.

There are 5 different movement types.

- *Normal Move*: Any model can move and turn in any direction up to his maximum M from its starting location. There is no minimal distance you have to keep models separate from each other.
- *Run Move*: Any model can move up to twice its maximum M. It can't climb or swim in the remaining turn. The model can do no other actions except the jump move.
- *Jump Move*: Any model can make a jump move during any Run or Normal move while using the maximum range for either Run or Move. It can jump half its M value horizontally. It can jump over any terrain or obstacles that are $1/4^{th}$ or smaller than his M. Any model can also jump down for half his M. If the model jumps down and the distance is more than half his M but beneath his maximum M movement the model takes a single wound. If the models falls more than his M he is mortally wounded.
  On a successful Agility check (roll a D6, if it's equal or lower than his agility it's a success) you may double the M value for all jump actions. The model can no longer shoot or take special actions.
- *Climb Move*: Any model can climb during it's normal Move. A climbing object can be climbed at full speed (rope, stairs, ladders etc) while a sheer surface can only be climbed at half speed. The model can no longer shoot or take special actions.
- *Swim Move*: Any model can swim up to half his maximum M. A model has to end its turn next to water to start swimming, and has to end its turn next to solid land to move out of it again next turn with their normal Move action (climb, jump etc). The model can no longer shoot or take special actions.

- *Disengage Combat*
  When a model is in base to base contact with an enemy model he can try to run away. He can only use his regular move, and any opponents model in base to base contact can make a single free attack.

The Shooting Phase

Range:

Each ranged weapon has a Range value. This is the maximum range any weapon can shoot. Targets beyond the maximum range value cannot be targeted.

Reload:

Each ranged weapon has a Reload Value. This is the numbers of turn needed to successfully reload the weapon so it can be shot again. Reloading takes the full turn of any model using it (so any model reloading can't fight, move or use a special ability). Most ranged weapons will have a Reload of 1 (so 1 turn).

Number of Shots:

Certain weapons (for example a brace of pistols) have 2 as its value for Number of Shots. This mean you can shoot twice with them at opponents models. When the total number of Number of Shots has been taken the weapon has to be reloaded. For example, shooting once with a brace of pistols means you can shoot one single shot again in the next turn before you need to reload. Both pistols are reloaded at the same time.

Targeting:

Each model equipped with shooting weapons can fire them during the shooting phase if **the model is not in base to base contact with an enemy model.**

Each model has an AIM value, which is the result needed on a D6 roll to decide if the model hits with its ranged weapon. For example, a goblin crewman has an AIM value of 4, meaning he hits his target on a 4 or higher on a single D6 roll. If the character has moved during the movement phase, the difficulty of hitting his target goes up, and the AIM value of the model increases by 1 (so if the goblin decided to walk up to his target to get in range, he now has a AIM of 5, and will hit on a 5 or 6).

Models can only shoot at a model that in is line of sight of themselves. You measure line of sight from the eyes from your model to any part of the opposing model (excluding it's base). If 50% of the model or more is covered by terrain or other models the aim value goes up by 1. If the model can't be seen at all, the shot cannot be made (so if the goblin decided to walk up to his target to get in range, and the target is also standing behind a low wall he now has a AIM of 6, and will hit on a 6… talk about needing goblin luck!).

Shooting into Combat:

If you are targeting a model that is in base to base contact with an opponent's model you must roll to hit as usual. Then number the number of models in contact with each other with your opponent and roll a D6 to see who gets actually hit. For example if 2 models are in contact, agree with your opponent that your model gets hit on 1-3 and his on 4-6. Then wound as normal.

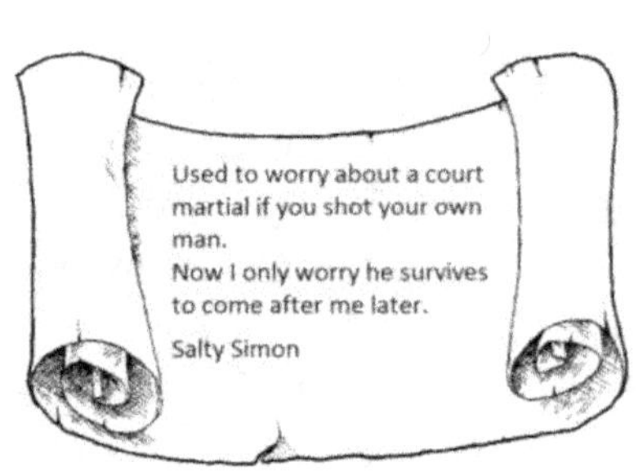

Wounding

If the shooting attack was successful, we need to make certain the pirate is actually hurt, and not just graced. Each shooting weapon has a base Strength value. Compare the strength value in the table beneath vs the targets resilience and roll a dice to check if the opponent is wounded (or dead).

Wound table	Resilience 1	Resilience 2	Resilience 3	Resilience 4	Resilience 5	Resilience 6
Strength 1	4+	5+	6+	6+	6+	6+
Strength 2	3+	4+	5+	6+	6+	6+
Strength 3	2+	3+	4+	5+	6+	6+
Strength 4	2+	2+	3+	4+	5+	6+
Strength 5	2+	2+	2+	3+	4+	5+
Strength 6	2+	2+	2+	2+	3+	4+
Strength 7	2+	2+	2+	2+	2+	3+
Strength 8	2+	2+	2+	2+	3+	2+

(For example, Biznit the Goblin Crewman has successfully shot a human with his lucky pistol. His pistol has a strength of 4, and his human opponent has a resilience of 3. This means that on a dice roll of 3+ or higher he has successfully wounded the opponent).

Each model has a Hitpoints Value (HP). Most models will either have 2 (regular crewman) or 3 (officers) hitpoints. Each time a model takes a wound place a wound marker next to it to indicate its lost hitpoint. When the model has 0 Hitpoints remove it from the table as it is mortally wounded.

Ranged Weapons:

Name Weapon	Range	Number of Shots	Strength	Reload
Single Pistol	8	1	4	1
Pair of Pistols	8	2	4	1
Grenade*	6	1	6 on target, 1 for each model with 3 inches from the hit model	Can only be fired once.
Javelins	6	1	Uses models strength	0
Bow	10	1	3	0
Long Rifle	16	1	5	2
Blunderbuss	6	1	5	1

***Grenades do not count to the maximum of 2 weapons per model. A model can only bring 2 grenades maximum to each game, and in case of a campaign, using a grenade means removing it from the model after the game.**

The Melee Phase

Any model that is close enough to an opponent's model can attack the opponent during the Melee phase. First you must determine if your models are close enough to actually fight. **A model that used a ranged weapon in the shooting phase turn, can't use a ranged weapon like a spear in the Melee phase.**

Range:

Close Combat weapons have a range value. If the value is C, it means your models bases have to touch the opponent's bases to attack them. This means that during the movement phase you have to move the base against the opponent's base. If the value is 1 or higher (for example a spear) this means you can attack the opponent if there is 1 inch or less between the bases.

Number of Attacks:

Certain weapons (for example 2 daggers) have +1 as their value for Number of Attacks. This means you can attack an additional time during Close Combat.

Strength Bonus:

Certain weapons (for example great weapons) have a strength bonus. Add this to the models Strength Value when looking at the Wound Chart.

Agility Penalty:

Certain weapons (for example great weapons) have an agility penalty. Detract this penalty from the models agility value when checking agility order.

If your model has no weapon equipped that can be used in close combat, the model must use their bare hands. They only get 1 attack in total, with -1 Agility, -1 Weapon skill and -1 Strength.

Order of Fighting:

Each model has its own Agility (A) value. During the Close Combat Phase, look at all the models that are in Combat Range of an enemy's model with your opponent. The model with the highest Agility (yours or the opponents) goes first, and then move on to the next highest agility etc until all models that are able to fight have attacked. If Agility Values are equal the models all attack at the same time (but roll them separately one at a time for clarity). If a model is killed at an earlier agility step he can no longer fight!

Attacking:

When your model attacks an opponent's model you get a single D6 to roll for each of its attacks value. Most models will have a single attack, but officers usually have 2 or more. Add any bonus attacks for the Number of Attacks special rule from its weapon. For example, Bork the Pirate has a 2 for its Attack value. He is also using 2 daggers, which gives him an additional attack, meaning Borks player gets 3 dice to roll for his attacks. Compare the attackers Weaponskill and the defenders Weaponskill between the models to see what you need to hit.

Weapon skill	Defenders 1	Defenders 2	Defenders 3	Defenders 4	Defenders 5	Defenders 6
Attacking 1	4+	4+	4+	5+	5+	5+
Attacking 2	3+	4+	5+	4+	5+	5+
Attacking 3	3+	3+	4+	4+	4+	5+
Attacking 4	3+	3+	3+	4+	4+	4+
Attacking 5	2+	3+	3+	3+	4+	4+
Attacking 6	2+	2+	3+	3+	3+	4+

Wounding

If the close combat attack was successful, we need to make certain the pirate is actually hurt, and not just graced. Each character has a base Strength value. Add any bonus from weapons to this value and compare the Strength value in the table beneath vs the targets Resilience and roll a dice to check if the opponent is wounded (or dead).

Wound table	Resilience 1	Resilience 2	Resilience 3	Resilience 4	Resilience 5	Resilience 6
Strength 1	4+	5+	6+	6+	6+	6+
Strength 2	3+	4+	5+	6+	6+	6+
Strength 3	2+	3+	4+	5+	6+	6+
Strength 4	2+	2+	3+	4+	5+	6+
Strength 5	2+	2+	2+	3+	4+	5+
Strength 6	2+	2+	2+	2+	3+	4+
Strength 7	2+	2+	2+	2+	2+	3+
Strength 8	2+	2+	2+	2+	3+	2+

(For example, Biznit the Goblin Crewman has successfully hit a human with one of his daggers. His base strength is 3, and the dagger gives no extra bonus, and his human opponent has a resilience of 3. This means that on a dice roll of 4+ or higher he has successfully wounded the opponent).

Each model has a Wound Value (W). Most models will either have 2 (regular crewman) or 3 (officers) hitpoints. Each time a model takes a wound place a wound marker next to it to indicate its lost wound. When the model has 0 Hitpoints remove it from the table as it is mortally wounded.

Close Combat Weapons:

Name Weapon:	Strength Modifier	Number of extra Attacks	Agility Modifier	Range
One handed Weapon (Axe/Sword/Mace etc.	0	0	0	C
Pair of One handed Weapons	0	1	0	C
Great Weapon	+2	0	-2	C
Pistol (used as melee club)	0	0	-1	C
Pair of Pistols (used as melee club)	0	1	-1	C
Spear	0	0	+1	1
Whip	-1	0	+2	1

Playing a Campaign

While playing a one off game can be fun as well, Pirate's Peril really becomes fun when playing in a Campaign with your friends. A campaign
gives your pirate band the chance to gain experience and new skills, as well as the opportunity to hire extra pirates after gathering treasure!

Starting a Campaign:
To start, you will need at least 2 players, but with everything piracy, the more pirates the better!
You can start a campaign as soon as at least 2 players have created their pirate bands, but new players can join the campaign any time they want. Although their bands will be weaker, they will quickly gain extra experience fighter the more seasoned Pirate Bands.

Playing a Campaign Game:
To start the campaign, the players select one of the scenarios to fight (see page 6). At
the end of each game the players work out how much experience their pirates have gained and
how many Treasure Tokens they received during the game.
If you are playing with more than 2 players you can either play the same game, with several players on the board, or switch opponents around each game so that everyone plays each other for a fixed number of games.

Winning a Campaign:
It's always good to set an end target for a campaign. You can either choose to agree on a fixed number of games, keep playing until someone earned X amount of Treasure or something else. Each Campaign group will want to do something different that suits their group, so make it clear with your group at the start of the campaign!

Post Battle:
After the battle is over, both players work their way through the following steps. The first 3 steps should be handled after the game when the players can check each other's results.
1. Check the Wounded
2. Award Experience
3. Selling Treasure
4. Buy new Equipment and Pirates

Check the Wounded:
Each model that was mortally wounded might be lucky enough to survive his or her wounds. This is called the Wounded Roll. Roll a D6 for each model that was mortally wounded. On a roll of 1, the model is permanently dead. One a roll of 2, the model is permanently wounded (roll the serious wounds chart). On a roll of 3-6 the model can fight again without any problems.

Coming back Stronger
If the model is a Crew Member, on a roll of 6 on a D6 for the Wounded Roll, roll another D6. If this roll is another 6, the Crew Member becomes an Officer model (he can gain experience from that point on, but keeps the old statistics).

Death of a Pirate:
When a Pirate is killed (Officer or Crew) all their weapons and equipment are also permanently lost.

Death of the Captain

If the Captain is killed you must either buy a new Captain, or nominate one of the officers to take his place (the officer keeps his old statistics/rules/equipment). If you can't afford a new captain, or have no officers, the Pirate Band suffers mutiny and is disbanded.

Disbanding a Pirate Band

You may disband your old Pirate Band at the end of any game and create a new one. The new Pirate Band starts again following the rules from 5.

You can also dismiss any Pirate in your Pirate Band at any time.

Serious Wound Chart:

1	Wooden Leg. The models movement is permanently reduced by 1.
2	Lost a Hand, gained a Hook. One of the weapons equipped on the model must be a one handed weapon.
3	Slow healing wound: The next game the model starts with 1 wound already taken.
4	Painful Scars: The models Agility is permanently reduced by 1.
5	Eye Patch: The models AIM value is reduced by 1.
6	Shaky Hands: Dealing with the pain made the Pirate addicted to strong liquor. The models Weaponskill value is reduced by 1.

Award Experience:

Experience fighting other pirates is tracked with Experience points which Officers can receive for surviving each game. When an Officer has gained 5 experience points they can increase their statistics or even possibly gain a new skill. This is repeated for every 5 experience points after this.

There are several ways to gain experience:

1. *Underdog Bonus:* Add up all your experience points in your crew and the number of models, vs your opponents crew combined experience plus his models. These numbers are your Pirate Band Rating (PBR).

If the difference in PRB is 10 or more each model gains an extra experience point.

If the difference in PRB is 20 or more each model gains 2 extra experience points.

If the difference in PRB is 30 or more each model gains 3 extra experience points.

2. *Surviving the game:* Each officer that survives gains one additional experience point.

3. *Winning the Game:* If you had the most treasure tokens at the end of the game your captain receives one additional experience point.

Write down the experience points for each officer on your campaign sheet. Crew Members don't acquire experience points unless they "Came Back Stronger".

Using experience:

If an officer gained 5 experience points he can roll on the Experience Charts.

Roll 2D6 and check the table for the result.

2	The model gains a permanent +1 to Resilience
3	The model gains a permanent +1 to Strength
4	The model may roll on the Skill Chart 1
5	he model gains a permanent +1 to Attack
6	The model gains a permanent +1 to Movement.
7	The model gains a permanent +1 to Agility
8	The model gains a permanent +1 to Weapon skill
9	The model gains a permanent +1 to Aim
10	The model may roll on the Skill Chart 2
11	The model gains a permanent extra Hitpoint.
12	You may choose which result in the table you want.

Each model can only receive each type of statistic increase only twice (so for example a maximum of +2 Strength. In case you roll the same result again, keep rolling until you receive a different result.

Skill Chart 1

1	**Devastating Charge**	
	In the first round of a combat if the model with this rule has moved in to base to base contact with an enemies the model gain +1 Attack.	
2	**Distracting**	
	Close Combat Attacks allocated at a model with this special rule suffer a -1 modifier when rolling to hit.	
3	**Far Jumper**	
	Models with this special rule gain a +2 on their Movement value when Jumping.	
4	**Frenzy**	
	Model parts with Frenzy gain +1 Attack, but can no longer use ranged weapons.	
5	**Hard Target**	
	Shooting Attacks targeting a model with this special rule suffer a -1 modifier when rolling to hit.	
6	**Hatred**	
	Model parts with this special rule may reroll failed to-hit rolls during the first Round of Combat.	

Skill Chart 2

1	**Lightning Reflexes**	
	Model parts with this special rule gain a +1 to-hit modifier to their Close Combat Attacks.	
2	**Monkey Climber**	
	Models with this special rule gain a +2 on their Movement value when climbing.	
3	**Nose for Treasure:**	
	If a model with this special rule ends the game without being mortally wounded, you may add 1 extra Treasure Token as a result for this game. You can never receive more than 6 Treasure Tokens at the end of a game though.	
4	**Quick to Fire**	
	Models with this special rule with this special rule don't suffer the -1 to-hit modifier for Moving and Shooting.	
5	**Scout**	
	Models with this special rule may deploy 8 inches from the table edge instead of 4.	
6	**Tough as Nails**	
	Models rolling to wound against a model with special rule receive a -1 penalty on their roll.	

Selling Treasure:

Keeping a Pirate Band running costs enough doubloons already for greedy pirates… and keeping the men happy is not cheap either. At the end of the game check how many Treasure Tokens you received, and compare it to the table for how much Doubloons you earned. The bigger the Pirate Band, the less you get!
Note the number of Doubloons you earned on your Campaign Sheet.

Number of Crew	1 Token	2 Tokens	3 Tokens	4 Tokens	5 Tokens	6 Tokens
1-3	10	20	30	40	50	60
4-6	8	18	28	38	48	58
7-9	6	16	26	36	46	56
10	4	14	24	34	44	54

Buying new equipment and Pirates.

Pirate Bands may purchase new equipment during games. Pirates can also swap equipment amongst themselves, or stash equipment in de Pirate Bands Storage which can equip other Pirates on a later date. You can only equip Pirates with the weapons listed for them in the Pirate Band List. Record any changes to the Pirates equipment on the Campaign Sheet.

Greenhide Pirate Band List

To an Orc, the world is one great arena within which they will try to prove themselves the finest combatant. While they won't shirk away from a fair fight, they are not averse to the additional fire weapons can offer. Goblins have some proportion of the same spirit, yet they will go to any lengths possible to have the advantage before risking combat. Besides Orcs and Goblins, they can also bring savage beasts called Gnashers to the table, and the scariest or craziest Pirate Bands have forced a Troll on their ship as a crew member.

Greenhide Pirate Bands are often seen as simple creatures, but they are often much more mobile than other pirates suspect with a baseline cunning equal to any man, and their volatile nature makes them Pirates to be feared.

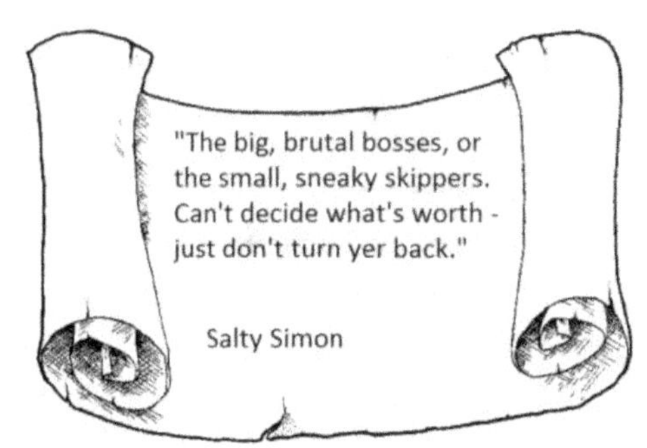

Orc Captain

Cost: 40 Doubloons

Special Rule: **Warcry**

Each model of the Greenhide Pirate Band increases their movement with +1 for one turn. One use only.

Movement	Strength	Resilience	Attack	Agility	Hitpoints	Aim	Weapon skill
4	5	4	2	4	3	3	5

Weapon options:

One Handed Weapon:	5 Doubloons	Pair of One Handed Weapons:	10 Doubloons
Great Weapon:	10 Doubloons	Pistol:	10 Doubloons
Pair of Pistols:	20 Doubloons		

Goblin Captain

Cost: 25 Doubloons

Special Rule: **Sneaky Sneaky**

During deployment, you may deploy 2 additional inches further from the board edge.

Movement	Strength	Resilience	Attack	Agility	Hitpoints	Aim	Weapon skill
4	4	4	2	4	3	4	4

Weapon options:

One Handed Weapon:	5 Doubloons	Pair of One Handed Weapons:	10 Doubloons
Great Weapon:	10 Doubloons	Pistol:	10 Doubloons
Pair of Pistols:	20 Doubloons		

Orc Officer

Cost: 20 Doubloons

Special Rule: **Bashing Order:**

A Orc Officer can smash some sense of Urgency in any of the Crew Members. All Crew member within 3 inches of an Orc Officer takes a wound if this ability is used, but gains a +2 bonus on movement for 2 turns.

Movement	Strength	Resilience	Attack	Agility	Hitpoints	Aim	Weapon skill
4	4	4	2	4	3	4	4

Weapon options:

One Handed Weapon:	5 Doubloons	Pair of One Handed Weapons:	10 Doubloons
Great Weapon:	10 Doubloons	Pistol:	10 Doubloons
Pair of Pistols:	20 Doubloons		

Goblin Officer
Cost: 15 Doubloons

Movement	Strength	Resilience	Attack	Agility	Hitpoints	Aim	Weapon skill
4	3	3	2	4	3	3	3

Weapon options:

One Handed Weapon:	*5 Doubloons*	*Pair of One Handed Weapons:*	*10 Doubloons*
Great Weapon:	*10 Doubloons*	*Pistol:*	*10 Doubloons*
Pair of Pistols:	*20 Doubloons*	*Grenade:*	*10 Doubloons*
Blunderbuss:	*20 Doubloons*		

Orc Crew Member
Cost: 10 Doubloons

Movement	Strength	Resilience	Attack	Agility	Hitpoints	Aim	Weapon skill
4	3	4	1	3	2	4	3

Weapon options:

One Handed Weapon:	*5 Doubloons*	*Pair of One Handed Weapons:*	*10 Doubloons*
Great Weapon:	*10 Doubloons*	*Pistol:*	*10 Doubloons*
Pair of Pistols:	*20 Doubloons*		

Goblin Crew Member
Cost: 6 Doubloons

Movement	Strength	Resilience	Attack	Agility	Hitpoints	Aim	Weapon skill
4	3	3	1	3	2	4	3

Weapon options:

One Handed Weapon:	*5 Doubloons*	*Pair of One Handed Weapons:*	*10 Doubloons*
Great Weapon:	*10 Doubloons*	*Pistol:*	*10 Doubloons*
Pair of Pistols:	*20 Doubloons*	*Grenade:*	*10 Doubloons*
Blunderbuss:	*20 Doubloons*		

Grotling Crew Member
Cost: 2 Doubloons

Movement	Strength	Resilience	Attack	Agility	Hitpoints	Aim	Weapon skill
4	2	2	1	3	1	3	2

One Handed Weapon: *5 Doubloons*

Gnasher Crew Member
Cost: 30 Doubloons

Special Rule: **Needs Supervision:**

A Gnasher Crew member is a simple beast.. if at the start of the movement phase the Gnasher is not within 4 inches of any Goblin or Orc Pirate model, the model can't move this turn.

Movement	Strength	Resilience	Attack	Agility	Hitpoints	Aim	Weapon skill
5	5	3	1	3	2	0	3

Giant Maw (counts as one handed weapon) Free

Troll Crew Member   Cost: 50 Doubloons

Special Rule: **Needs Supervision:**

A Troll Crew member is a simple beast.. if at the start of the movement phase the Troll is not within 4 inches of any Goblin or Orc Pirate model, the model can't move this turn.

Movement	Strength	Resilience	Attack	Agility	Hitpoints	Aim	Weapon skill
4	5	4	3	3	3	0	3

One handed Weapon: *5 Doubloons*   *Acid Belch**   *Free*

Acid Puke is a special ranged weapon that only the Troll can use.

Name Weapon	Range	Number of Shots	Strength	Reload
Acid Belch	4	1	5	0

Vampire Pirate Band List

Across the world, beneath the veneer of civilization, vampires have worked under a cloak of shadow, turning death from an affliction to a weapon. Theirs is not a mere return to past life, instead they linger unchanged while turning the corpses of their foes into weapons of horrifying destruction.

The life of a Pirate suits them, combining their natural bloodthirst with the safety of being hard to track to make them lethal killers on the Sea.

They are supported by their Necromancers and their undead minions, taking more than just gold from their victims.

Vampire Captain
Cost: 60 Doubloons

Special Rule: **Bloodthirst**

Each time a Vampire Captain wounds an enemies model, he regains a single lost wound.

Movement	Strength	Resilience	Attack	Agility	Hitpoints	Aim	Weapon skill
5	5	5	3	5	3	3	6

Weapon options:

One Handed Weapon:	*5 Doubloons*	*Pair of One Handed Weapons:*	*10 Doubloons*
Great Weapon:	*10 Doubloons*	*Whip:*	*15 Doubloons*
Pistol:	*10 Doubloons*	*Pair of Pistols:*	*20 Doubloons*

Necromancer Officer
Cost: 30 Doubloons

Special Rule: **Raise the Dead**

At the end of the Movement Phase, a Necromancer may heal a single wound from any model within 6 inches.

Movement	Strength	Resilience	Attack	Agility	Hitpoints	Aim	Weapon skill
4	3	3	1	3	2	4	3

Weapon options:

One Handed Weapon:	*5 Doubloons*	*Pair of One Handed Weapons:*	*10 Doubloons*
Whip:	*10 Doubloons*	*Spear:*	*10 Doubloons*

Undead Officer
Cost: 20 Doubloons

Special Rule: **Undead Resistance**

It's tricky to wound the undead thanks to the lack of working internal organs. Whenever a model with this rule takes a wound, roll a D6. On a natural roll of a 6, the model doesn't take the wound.

Movement	Strength	Resilience	Attack	Agility	Hitpoints	Aim	Weapon skill
4	4	4	2	2	3	4	4

Weapon options:

One Handed Weapon:	*5 Doubloons*	*Pair of One Handed Weapons:* 10 Doubloons

Great Weapon: *10 Doubloons*   *Spear:*   *10 Doubloons*

Zombie Crew Member
Cost: 6 Doubloons

Special Rule: **Undead Resistance**

It's tricky to wound the undead thanks to the lack of working internal organs. Whenever a model with this rule takes a wound, roll a D6. On a natural roll of a 6, the model doesn't take the wound.

Movement	Strength	Resilience	Attack	Agility	Hitpoints	Aim	Weapon skill
4	3	3	1	1	2	5	2

Weapon options:

One Handed Weapon:	*5 Doubloons*	*Pair of One Handed Weapons:*	*10 Doubloons*
Spear:	*10 Doubloons*	*Pistol:*	*8 Doubloons*
Pair of Pistols:	*16 Doubloons*		

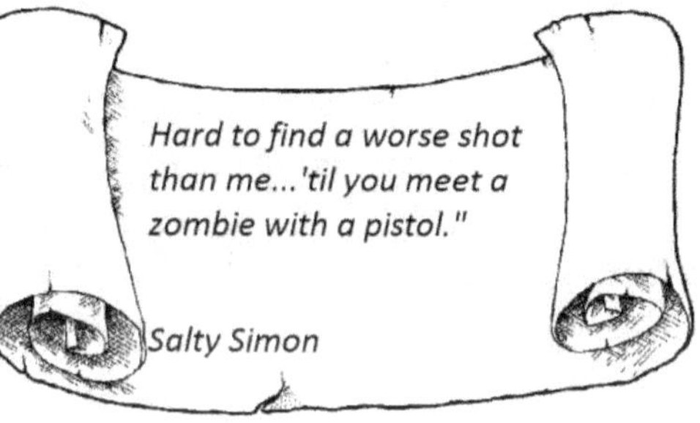

Ghoul Crew Member
Cost: 25 Doubloons

Special Rule: **Poison**

Eating the dead as their favorite food, has turned the body of the Ghouls into a breeding pit of disease and poison. Whenever a Ghoul rolls a natural 6 to hit, he automatically wounds the opponents model.

Movement	Strength	Resilience	Attack	Agility	Hitpoints	Aim	Weapon skill
4	3	4	1	3	2	4	3

Weapon options:

Claws (count as : Pair of One Handed Weapons):   *free*

Undead Hound/Crew Member
Cost: 5 Doubloons

Special Rule: **Undead Resistance**

It's tricky to wound the undead thanks to the lack of working internal organs. Whenever a model with this rule takes a wound, roll a D6. On a natural roll of a 6, the model doesn't take the wound.

Movement	Strength	Resilience	Attack	Agility	Hitpoints	Aim	Weapon skill
7	3	3	1	2	1	5	3

Bite Attack (count as: one handed weapon)   *free*

Dwarf Pirates

For most Dwarfs, life is lived on the very earth where they feel a strong connection though. This means that those Dwarfs that take to the Sea are a very special kind of dwarf, or as some call it, flat out crazy. Dwarf Pirate Bands are often small, but each dwarf is though, and usually armed with some of the best weapons available, and supported by their engineers they can bring death from quite a distance. Some Seekers also join the Pirate Bands, bringing a very sharp close combat edge to any group of dwarven pirates.

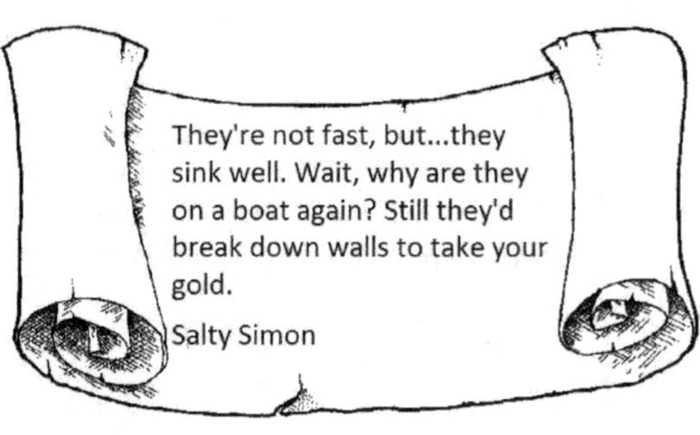

Dwarf Captain

Cost: 45 Doubloons

Special Rule: **Tough as Iron**

Dwarfs have a proud tradition to resist the worst the world can throw at them. Once a game, at the start of any players turn, the Dwarf Captain can inspire his crew with tales of dwarven resistance. Every model within 6 inches of the Dwarf Captain (excluding himself) have +1 Resilience until the end of the players turn.

Movement	Strength	Resilience	Attack	Agility	Hitpoints	Aim	Weapon skill
3	4	5	2	3	3	3	5

Weapon options:

One Handed Weapon:	5 Doubloons	Pair of One Handed Weapons:	10 Doubloons
Great Weapon:	10 Doubloons	Pistol:	10 Doubloons
Pair of Pistols:	20 Doubloons	Grenade:	10 Doubloons
Blunderbuss:	20 Doubloons		

Dwarf Officer

Cost: 22 Doubloons

Special Rule: **Steady Defense**

Whenever a Dwarf Officer model moves out of combat, opposing models do not get a free attack.

Movement	Strength	Resilience	Attack	Agility	Hitpoints	Aim	Weapon skill
3	4	4	2	3	3	4	5

Weapon options:

One Handed Weapon:	5 Doubloons	Pair of One Handed Weapons:	10 Doubloons
Great Weapon:	10 Doubloons	Pistol:	10 Doubloons
Pair of Pistols:	20 Doubloons	Grenade:	10 Doubloons
Blunderbuss:	20 Doubloons		

Dwarf Engineer   Cost: 20 Doubloons

Special Rule: **Upgrades!**

Any Pirate Band that has a Dwarf Engineer in its crew at the start of the game, gains a +2 range bonus on all their ranged weapons (excluding grenades), thanks to the tinkering of the Engineer.

Movement	Strength	Resilience	Attack	Agility	Hitpoints	Aim	Weapon skill
3	3	4	2	2	3	3	4

One Handed Weapon:	*5 Doubloons*	*Pair of One Handed Weapons:*	*10 Doubloons*
Great Weapon:	*10 Doubloons*	*Pistol:*	*10 Doubloons*
Pair of Pistols:	*20 Doubloons*	*Grenade:*	*10 Doubloons*
Blunderbuss:	*20 Doubloons*	*Long Rifle*	*20 Doubloons*

Seeker Crew   Cost: 15 Doubloons

Special Rule: **Vengeful strike**

Whenever a Seeker takes a wound from a model, he gets a single free attack back if the Seeker has not attacked this turn yet.

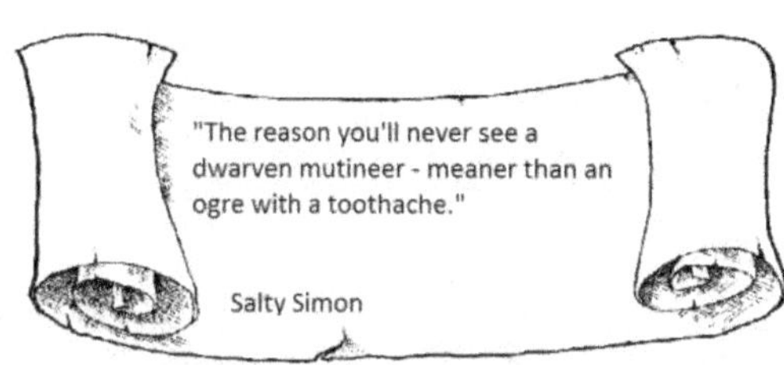

Movement	Strength	Resilience	Attack	Agility	Hitpoints	Aim	Weapon skill
3	3	4	1	2	2	4	4

Weapon options:

One Handed Weapon:	*5 Doubloons*	*Pair of One Handed Weapons:*	*10 Doubloons*
Great Weapon:	*10 Doubloons*	*Pistol:*	*10 Doubloons*
Pair of Pistols:	*20 Doubloons*		

Dwarf Crew Member   Cost: 10 Doubloons

Movement	Strength	Resilience	Attack	Agility	Hitpoints	Aim	Weapon skill
3	3	4	1	2	2	4	4

One Handed Weapon:	*5 Doubloons*	*Pair of One Handed Weapons:*	*10 Doubloons*
Great Weapon:	*10 Doubloons*	*Pistol:*	*10 Doubloons*
Pair of Pistols:	*20 Doubloons*	*Grenade:*	*10 Doubloons*
Blunderbuss:	*20 Doubloons*	*Long Rifle*	*20 Doubloons*

Human Pirates

Humans are the most dominant type of Pirate, and Pirate victim. Lacking the toughness of the Dwarves, or the ferocity of the Greenskins, the Humans strength lies in numbers and teamwork, combined with their mastery of ranged weapons to shore up their weaknesses.

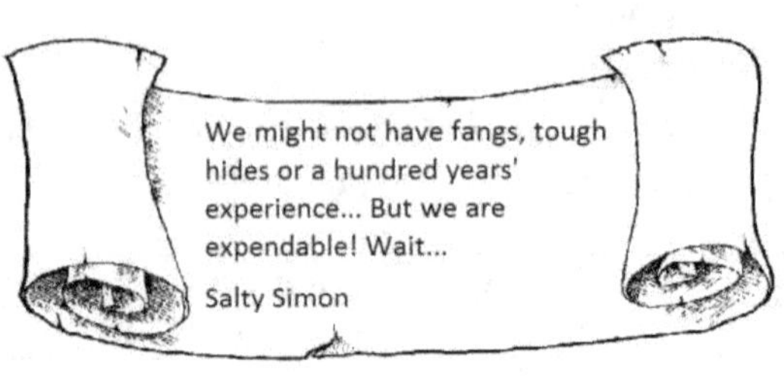

Human Captain
Cost: 35 Doubloons

Special Rule: **Inspiring Presence**

At the start of their turn a human captain may inspire one of his pirates. A single model with 6 inches of the Captain either gains +2 agility, +2 movement or -1 Aim until the end of the players turn.

Movement	Strength	Resilience	Attack	Agility	Hitpoints	Aim	Weapon skill
4	4	4	2	4	3	3	5

Weapon options:

One Handed Weapon:	*5 Doubloons*	*Pair of One Handed Weapons:*	*10 Doubloons*
Great Weapon:	*10 Doubloons*	*Pistol:*	*10 Doubloons*
Pair of Pistols:	*20 Doubloons*	*Grenade:*	*10 Doubloons*
Blunderbuss:	*20 Doubloons*		

Human Officer
Cost: 20 Doubloons

Movement	Strength	Resilience	Attack	Agility	Hitpoints	Aim	Weapon skill
4	4	4	2	3	3	3	4

Weapon options:

Weapon options:

One Handed Weapon:	*5 Doubloons*	*Pair of One Handed Weapons:*	*10 Doubloons*
Great Weapon:	*10 Doubloons*	*Pistol:*	*10 Doubloons*
Pair of Pistols:	*20 Doubloons*	*Grenade:*	*10 Doubloons*
Blunderbuss:	*20 Doubloons*	*Whip:*	*20 Doubloons*

Pistelero Officer
Cost: 25 Doubloons

Special Rule: **Rapid Shot**

Pistelero Officers have mastered the art of rapid reloading their pair of pistols. They can take a +1 Penalty on Aim for a turn when shooting to reduce the reload value of their Pistols by 1 (meaning they can shoot both pistols again next turn).

Movement	Strength	Resilience	Attack	Agility	Hitpoints	Aim	Weapon skill
4	3	4	2	2	3	3	4

Weapon options:

Pair of Pistols: *20 Doubloons*

Human Crew Member   Cost: 6 Doubloons

Movement	Strength	Resilience	Attack	Agility	Hitpoints	Aim	Weapon skill
4	3	3	1	3	2	4	3

Weapon options:

One Handed Weapon:	*5 Doubloons*	*Pair of One Handed Weapons:*	*10 Doubloons*
Spear	*10 Doubloons*	*Pistol:*	*10 Doubloons*
Pair of Pistols:	*20 Doubloons*		

Rifle Crew Member   Cost: 6 Doubloons

Movement	Strength	Resilience	Attack	Agility	Hitpoints	Aim	Weapon skill
4	3	3	1	3	2	4	3

Weapon options:

One Handed Weapon:	*5 Doubloons*	*Long Rifle*	*20 Doubloons*

Assistant Rifle Crew Member   Cost: 6 Doubloons

Special Rule: **Helping Reload**

If at the start of the shooting phase, an assistant rifle crew member is in base to base contact with a Rifle Crew Member he can help reload their Rifle, reducing the Long Rifle reload value by 1 for each Assistant Rifle Crew Member in base to base contact to a maximum of 0.

Movement	Strength	Resilience	Attack	Agility	Hitpoints	Aim	Weapon skill
4	3	3	1	3	2	4	3

Weapon options:

One Handed Weapon: *5 Doubloons*

Seasoned Crew Member   Cost: 12 Doubloons

Movement	Strength	Resilience	Attack	Agility	Hitpoints	Aim	Weapon skill
4	4	3	1	3	2	4	4

Weapon options:

One Handed Weapon:	*5 Doubloons*	*Pair of One Handed Weapons:*	*10 Doubloons*
Spear	*10 Doubloons*	*Pistol:*	*10 Doubloons*
Pair of Pistols:	*20 Doubloons*	*Blunderbuss*	*20 Doubloons*
Grenade:	*10 Doubloons*		

Elven Pirates

Almost as diverse as the Human Pirate Bands, many types of Elves live the Buccaneers life. From the Dread Elves, seeking treasure and slaves, to the rarer Highborn Elves, who mostly use the pirate life to escape Highborn society. While culturally different, they are all equally dangerous, on land and sea.

Divided we Stand

All Elf Pirate Bands start with either a Highborn Captain , or a Dread Captain. Once chosen, any replacement captain must be the same type. A pirate Highborn lead band may only take Crew Members and officers with the Highborn name included, and Dread lead bands, may only take Crew Members and officers with the Dread name included.

Highborn Captain

Cost: 50 Doubloons

Special Rule: **Guiding Hand**

All elven models in a Pirate Band that is led by a Highborn Captain gain the Lightning Reflexes special rule.

Movement	Strength	Resilience	Attack	Agility	Hitpoints	Aim	Weapon skill
5	4	3	2	6	3	3	6

Weapon options:

One Handed Weapon:	*5 Doubloons*	*Pair of One Handed Weapons:*	*10 Doubloons*
Spear	*10 Doubloons*	*Bow*	*10 Doubloons*
Great Weapon	*10 Doubloons*		

Dread Captain

Cost: 55 Doubloons

Special Rule: **Dread & Hatred**

All elven models in a Pirate Band that is led by a Dread Captain gains the Hatred Special Rule. They may also reroll results of 1 on the dice for close combat attacks.

Movement	Strength	Resilience	Attack	Agility	Hitpoints	Aim	Weapon skill
5	4	3	2	6	3	3	6

Weapon options:

One Handed Weapon:	*5 Doubloons*	*Pair of One Handed Weapons:*	*10 Doubloons*
Crossbow (counts as single pistol)	*10 Doubloons*	*Repeating Crossbow (counts as double pistol)*	*20 Doubloons*
Great Weapon	*10 Doubloons*	*Whip*	*20 Doubloons*

Elf Officer

Cost: 25 Doubloons

Movement	Strength	Resilience	Attack	Agility	Hitpoints	Aim	Weapon skill
5	4	3	2	5	3	3	5

Weapon options:

One Handed Weapon:	*5 Doubloons*	*Pair of One Handed Weapons:*	*10 Doubloons*
Crossbow (counts as single pistol)	*10 Doubloons*	*Repeating Crossbow (counts as double pistol)*	*10 Doubloons*
Great Weapon	*10 Doubloons*	*Bow*	*10 Doubloons*

Elf Blade Specialist Crew Member   Cost: 18 Doubloons

Movement	Strength	Resilience	Attack	Agility	Hitpoints	Aim	Weapon skill
5	3	3	1	5	2	4	6

Weapon options:

One Handed Weapon: 5 Doubloons   *Pair of One Handed Weapon:*   10 Doubloons

Great Weapon   10 Doubloons

Dread Elf Crew Member   Cost: 15 Doubloons

Movement	Strength	Resilience	Attack	Agility	Hitpoints	Aim	Weapon skill
5	3	3	1	5	2	3	5

One Handed Weapon: 5 Doubloons   *Pair of One Handed Weapons:*   10 Doubloons

Crossbow (counts as single pistol)   10 Doubloons   *Repeating Crossbow (counts as double pistol)* 20 Doubloons

Great Weapon   10 Doubloons   *Whip*

Highborn Crew Member   Cost: 15 Doubloons

Movement	Strength	Resilience	Attack	Agility	Hitpoints	Aim	Weapon skill
5	3	3	1	5	2	3	5

Weapon options:

One Handed Weapon: 5 Doubloons   *Pair of One Handed Weapons:*   10 Doubloons

Spear   10 Doubloons   *Bow*   10 Doubloons

Great Weapon   10 Doubloons

Highborn Scout Crew Member   Cost: 20 Doubloons

Special Rule: **Scout**

Highborn Scouts may deploy 8 inches from the table edge.

Movement	Strength	Resilience	Attack	Agility	Hitpoints	Aim	Weapon skill
5	3	3	1	5	2	3	5

Weapon options:

One Handed Weapon: 5 Doubloons   *Pair of One Handed Weapons:*   10 Doubloons

Spear   10 Doubloons   *Bow*   10 Doubloons

Great Weapon   10 Doubloons

Dread Elf Corsair Crew Member   Cost: 20 Doubloons

Special Rule: **Slave masters**

Dread Elf Corsairs are masters in taking Slaves alive. Each enemy model that was mortally wounded by a Dread Elf Corsair as the final wound adds 2 extra doubloons at the end of the game.

Movement	Strength	Resilience	Attack	Agility	Hitpoints	Aim	Weapon skill
5	3	3	1	5	2	3	5

One Handed Weapon: 5 Doubloons   *Pair of One Handed Weapons:*   10 Doubloons

Crossbow (counts as single pistol)   10 Doubloons   *Whip*   20 Doubloons

Ogre Pirates

One of the rarest and most feared sights on the Archipelago are the Ogre Pirate Bands. Most are former Iron Crown mercenaries who decided to start on their own after stealing a seaworthy vessel and joining forces. While they often struggle with their sizes in the ruins, any other pirate band caught in the open facing them has a serious problem!

Big Pirates on Little Boats
An Ogre Pirate Band has a maximum of 7 models. More would simply not fit on their stolen boats!

Ogre Captain   Cost: 55 Doubloons
Special Rule: **Eaten his way to the Top**
Ogre Captains usually gain their position after killing and eating the previous Captain in a challenge, resulting in the type of leader that always make certain his men are well fed… usually by feeding them the opposition.
Whenever a model is deadly wounded by the Ogre Captain roll a D6. On a 4 or higher, all Ogre Pirates within 8 inches gain a plus 1 bonus to their Attack and Weapon skill value, as the prospect of fresh meet encourages them, until the end of the next round.

Movement	Strength	Resilience	Attack	Agility	Hitpoints	Aim	Weapon skill
5	5	5	2	3	4	4	4

Weapon options:

One Handed Weapon:	5 Doubloons	Pair of One Handed Weapons:	10 Doubloons
Great Weapon:	10 Doubloons	Pistol:	10 Doubloons
Pair of Pistols:	20 Doubloons		

Ogre Officer   Cost: 45 Doubloons
Special Rule: **Ogre Rage**
Whenever an Ogre officer loses a hitpoint, roll a D6. On a 4 or higher they gain an extra attack in the next melee phase.

Movement	Strength	Resilience	Attack	Agility	Hitpoints	Aim	Weapon skill
5	4	4	2	3	4	4	4

Weapon options:

One Handed Weapon:	5 Doubloons	Pair of One Handed Weapons:	10 Doubloons
Great Weapon:	10 Doubloons	Pistol:	10 Doubloons
Pair of Pistols:	20 Doubloons		

Ogre Crew Member   Cost: 25 Doubloons

Movement	Strength	Resilience	Attack	Agility	Hitpoints	Aim	Weapon skill
5	4	4	1	2	3	4	3

Weapon options:

One Handed Weapon:	5 Doubloons	Pair of One Handed Weapons:	10 Doubloons
Great Weapon:	10 Doubloons		

Experienced Ogre Crew Member   Cost: 35 Doubloons

Movement	Strength	Resilience	Attack	Agility	Hitpoints	Aim	Weapon skill
5	4	4	2	3	3	4	4

Weapon options:

One Handed Weapon:	*5 Doubloons*	*Pair of One Handed Weapons:*	*10 Doubloons*
Great Weapon:	*10 Doubloons*	*Pistol:*	*10 Doubloons*
Pair of Pistols:	*20 Doubloons*		

Ogre Bombardier Member   Cost: 30 Doubloons

Special Rule: **Clubs and Cups**

An Ogre Bombardier has no problem using his Blunderbuss in melee as well as he uses it for shooting.

He may use the Blunderbuss as a Great Weapon in the melee phase.

Movement	Strength	Resilience	Attack	Agility	Hitpoints	Aim	Weapon skill
5	4	4	1	2	3	4	3

Weapon options:

Blunderbuss: *20 Doubloons*

Campaign Sheet

Name Pirate Band:	
Remaining Doubloons:	
Pirate Storage:	

Name Pirate: ________________

Type: ________________ Officer/Crew ________________

Equipment: ____

Special Rules: ____

Movement	Strength	Resilience	Attack	Agility	Hitpoints	Aim	Weapon skill	Experience

----

Name Pirate: ________________

Type: ________________ Officer/Crew ________________

Equipment: ____

Special Rules: ____

Movement	Strength	Resilience	Attack	Agility	Hitpoints	Aim	Weapon skill	Experience

----

Name Pirate: ________________

Type: ________________ Officer/Crew ________________

Equipment: ____

Special Rules: ____

Movement	Strength	Resilience	Attack	Agility	Hitpoints	Aim	Weapon skill	Experience

----

Name Pirate: ________________

Type: ________________ Officer/Crew ________________

Equipment: ____

Special Rules: ____

Movement	Strength	Resilience	Attack	Agility	Hitpoints	Aim	Weapon skill	Experience

----

Name Pirate: ________________

Type: _______________ Officer/Crew _______________

Equipment: _____________________________________

Special Rules: _____________________________________

Movement	Strength	Resilience	Attack	Agility	Hitpoints	Aim	Weapon skill	Experience

----

Name Pirate: ________________

Type: _______________ Officer/Crew _______________

Equipment: _____________________________________

Special Rules: _____________________________________

Movement	Strength	Resilience	Attack	Agility	Hitpoints	Aim	Weapon skill	Experience

----

Name Pirate: ________________

Type: _______________ Officer/Crew _______________

Equipment: _____________________________________

Special Rules: _____________________________________

Movement	Strength	Resilience	Attack	Agility	Hitpoints	Aim	Weapon skill	Experience

----

Name Pirate: ________________

Type: _______________ Officer/Crew _______________

Equipment: _____________________________________

Special Rules: _____________________________________

Movement	Strength	Resilience	Attack	Agility	Hitpoints	Aim	Weapon skill	Experience

----

Name Pirate: ________________

Type: _______________ Officer/Crew _______________

Equipment: _____________________________________

Special Rules: _____________________________________

Movement	Strength	Resilience	Attack	Agility	Hitpoints	Aim	Weapon skill	Experience

----

How to build a Pirate's Peril table

Size of the table:
We advice to have a 4 by 4 table for most games of Pirate's Peril.

Terrain:
As a Skirmish Game, Pirate's Peril works best with enough terrain to spice up any battle. Since the setting takes place in an old pirate city you can use a lot of buildings and wreckage on the table to create cover, to create a more exciting game where maneuvering becomes vital to the success of any pirate band. Especially buildings with several floors can have a big impact on any game.
With the climb move action any stairs or ropes become a viable way to go up, or even just sheer climbing, and the jump move makes it possible to even jump from building to building.

We advise any table to have at least 8 to 10 pieces of Terrain that aren't just flat surface to play on, and don't forget to add some simple water features and trees to make this easier to start collecting your terrain.

Special Terrain:
Here are some example rules for special terrain for your games. Don't forget you can create your own terrain rules as well, to better fit your custom terrain pieces.

Burning Building:
At the end of each turn, each model inside of a burning building is hit by a strength 3 hit.

Corpse Pile
All models except members of the Vampire Pirate Band have a risk of disease when being in contact with one of the many corpse piles left after the flood. Every model that has been in with 2 inches of a Corpse Pile must roll a D6 at the end of each game. On a roll of a 6 it's resilience permanently lowered by 1.

Dense Forest:
Where regular trees give standard cover, this terrain piece makes a model not viewable for any ranged attacks. The model itself takes a -1 on all of his own ranged attacks.

Paved Road:
All movement (per inch) on a Paved Road is multiplied by 1.5 when using standard movement or running.

QuickSand:
When ever a model moves inside of Quicksand terrain he must make a agility check. If the roll is higher than it's inative he can't move any further this turn.

Strong Current:
Water terrain features with the Strong Current reduce any swimming distances by another 50%

Swamp:
All movement inside Swampy terrain is halved.

Designer notes

This game will always have a unique place in my heart, and I am quite happy to be able to share it now.
It has grown out of the games I played at home, with my young son who wanted to join in the fun of Wargaming,
while not being of an age where regular games of T9A were a real option (although, the happy moment where he
can finally start playing with his own Saurian Army is coming closer and closer!)
As a result, this game is quite simple in how it plays out, since the rules were partly designed with the feedback of
a 7 year old boy, and it's main focus is on being easy to pick up for those with less experience with massive scale
miniature wargaming.

While this is still just the Beta version of the rulepack, I hope people will give it a try, and give me feedback on
things that can be improved, just as long as the spirit of the original game I played with my son remain. Cool
fantasy pirates, that can be played with the models you already have at home, or where you can create small
unique pirate bands without spending months painting miniatures. Anyone can reach me on the Ninth Age Forum,
so send me a pm if you want to talk like a pirate!

I am aware that not every T9A army has a pirate band counterpart yet, and that is mostly done on purpose for
now, since we will include those in the extra material that will be released in the future. I for one, can't wait to
convert the upcoming Infernal Dwarf book to a cool pirate band.

All that is left is to thank my fellow T9A members who helped me out with this book, and ofcourse my son Roland
for being the first playtester of this game. Special thanks to Edward as well who helped me out with giving this
game some official (and unique) Ninth age background material.

I hope to have the full versions, and the first expansion out somewhere before the end of the year, but for now,
please load your pistols, grab your pirate hats and go hunt for some treasure and play this game!

Blonde Beer

Compatible with
IX
AGE
TM
The 9th Age™

www.ingramcontent.com/pod-product-compliance
Lightning Source LLC
LaVergne TN
LVHW080613200726
843509LV00007B/304